P9-CCX-094

To the Bellevue Art Museum
supporters who made it possible
for me to meet Kerry Wade
J. S. W.

For Matt and Barry
D. R.

Text copyright © 2007 by Janet S. Wong
Illustrations copyright © 2007 by David Roberts

All rights reserved. No part of this book may be
reproduced, transmitted, or stored in an information
retrieval system in any form or by any means,
graphic, electronic, or mechanical, including
photocopying, taping, and recording, without prior
written permission from the publisher.

First edition 2007

Library of Congress Cataloging-in-Publication Data
is available.

Library of Congress Catalog Card Number 2006049075

ISBN 978-0-7636-2380-7

2 4 6 8 10 9 7 5 3 1

Printed in China

This book was typeset in Handwriter.
The illustrations were done in watercolor and ink.

Candlewick Press
2067 Massachusetts Avenue
Cambridge, Massachusetts 02140

visit us at www.candlewick.com

The
DUMPSTER
DIVER

CANDLEWICK PRESS
CAMBRIDGE, MASSACHUSETTS

JANET S WONG

illustrated by
DAVID ROBERTS

Central Rappahannock Regional Library
1201 Caroline Street
Fredericksburg, VA 22401

16 OZ

Anyone knows you can

dive for treasure in the ocean,

but our neighbor

**Steve** the Electrician dives for buried treasure **RIGHT SMACK HERE** in our backstreet alley.

Once a month during **fall** and winter and spring,

and **every week** in the summertime,

Steve slinks into the

**basement storage room.**

Five minutes later,

the **DUMPSTER DIVER** comes out.

When Steve is ready to dive he taps five times on my bedroom window.

I wave to Steve and knock on Johnny's wall. Johnny hops to his window and shouts upstairs to Lina on the third floor.

and the DIVING TEAM is ready to go.

I am

HOSE HANDLER #1

(also known as the Nozzler).   Lina is

HOSE HANDLER #2

(also known as the Snake Charmer).

Johnny is the

FAUCETEER.

Steve climbs up the back-alley wall, picks a Dumpster, and dives in.

Beetles and roaches and spiders splash out.

I never imagined

there were so many millions of legs

living two hundred feet away from me.

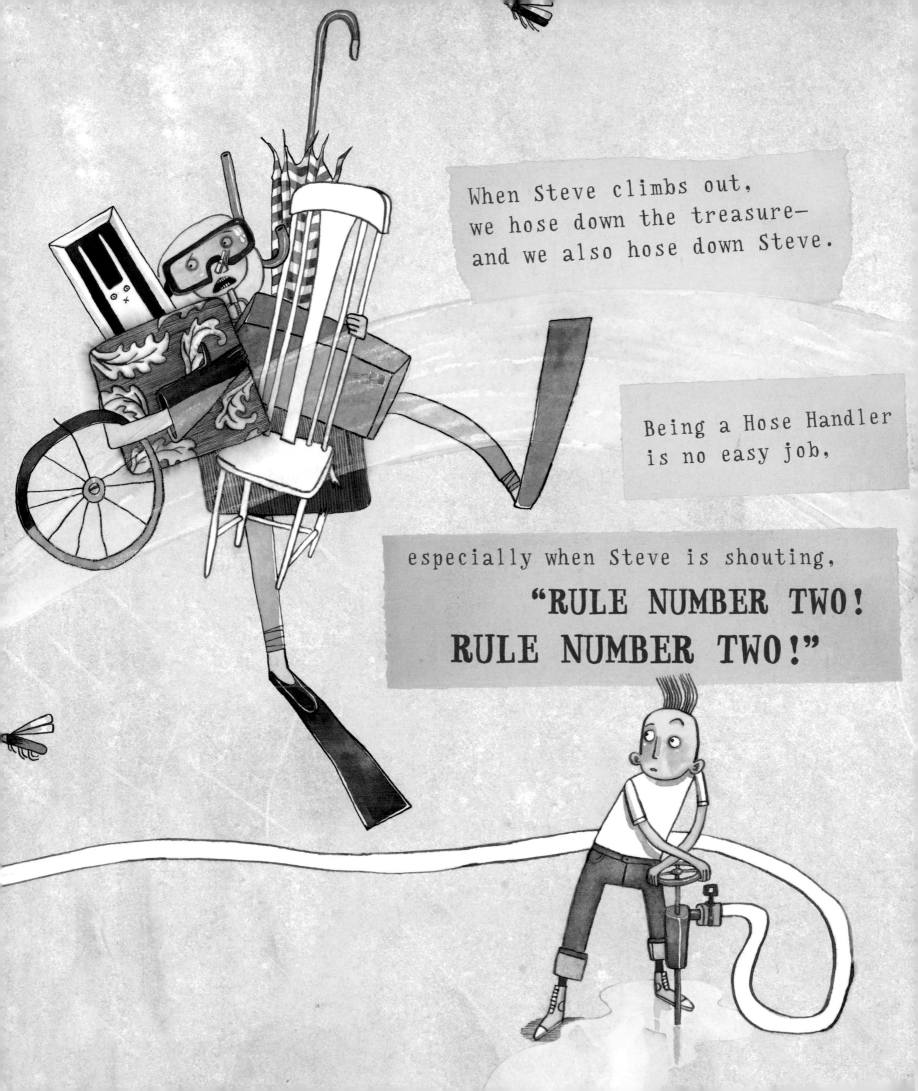

When Steve climbs out,
we hose down the treasure—
and we also hose down Steve.

Being a Hose Handler
is no easy job,

especially when Steve is shouting,

**"RULE NUMBER TWO!
RULE NUMBER TWO!"**

Thursday is **TRASH DAY**, but we do our real work on weekends. Last Saturday we started with a pair of busted skis.

Johnny drew,

Lina measured,

I drilled holes

for nuts and bolts,

Steve cut with a saw,

and soon we had

a PARASKATER!

**An old blender**

**can become a lamp.**

**An old lamp**

**can become a table.**

And an old table
plus two banged-up skateboards
plus a ripped crib mattress
plus a hand-held shower
plus thirty-two screws and a roll of duct tape can become

anything we want it to be.

Yesterday's TREASURE OF THE DAY

was an old computer

that almost became a flowerpot (Johnny's idea)

or a fish tank (Lina's idea)

The Grouch (who lives next door to Steve) says Steve is crazy—too lazy to work hard to make enough money to buy new stuff at the store like good people should.

She says his apartment is

FULL OF JUNK !

The Grouch says we kids better watch out or we'll get cut up from the trash.

But it was Steve who got cut up on broken glass and rusted metal when the Dumpster trash collapsed under him.

SERVES YOU RIGHT! WHAT DO YOU EXPECT, DIGGING THROUGH THE TRASH?

The Grouch has a point. Starting today, we are going to stop digging through the trash.

Starting today, we are going to knock on every door in our apartment building,

collecting our own special Dumpster-Diver Useful Junk.

Starting today, we are going to put our Useful Junk carefully in the basement storage room.

Except, maybe, for this **old wagon**

and that **broken rocker,**

this **tennis racket** and that **popcorn machine**—

all the stuff we need . . . .